THiS BOOK SUCKS

CREATED BY MIKE JUDGE

WRITTEN BY
SAM JOHNSON AND CHRIS MARCIL

MTV BOOKS / CALLAWAY / POCKET BOOKS

Beavis and Butt-head are not role models. They're not even human.
They're cartoons. Some of the things they do would cause a real person
to get hurt, expelled, arrested, possibly deported.
To put it another way: Don't try this at home.

This book was produced by Callaway Editions, Inc.
54 Seventh Avenue South, New York, NY 10014,
under the direction of Nicholas Callaway, Editorial Director,
and Charles Melcher, Publisher.

Editor: Glenn Eichler
Art Direction: Reiner Design Consultants, Inc.
Illustrators: Michael A. Baez, Bryon Moore, Ben Price, and Barry Vodos
Colorist: Karen Hyden
Director of Production: True Sims
Editorial Assistant: Courtney Howell
Production Assistant: José Rodriguez

Special thanks at MTV to: Joy Marcus, Judy McGrath, Ed Paparo, Lisa Silfen,
Abby Terkuhle, and Van Toffler.

Special thanks at Pocket Books to: Peter Anderson, Gina Centrello, Bill Grose,
Anne Maitland, Judith Regan, Jack Romanos, Walter Walker, and Kara Welsh.

Photo Credits: p.9: UPI/Bettmann; p.22: UPI/Bettmann Newsphotos;
p.44: AP/Wide World Photos; p.58: AP/Wide World Photos;
p.68: The Bettmann Archive; p.72: Ewing Galloway, Inc.;
p.88: FPG International Corp.; p.92: AP/Wide World Photos.

An *Original* Publication of MTV Books/Callaway/Pocket Books

POCKET BOOKS, a division of Simon & Schuster Inc.
1230 Avenue of the Americas, New York, NY 10020

Library of Congress Cataloging–in–Publication Number: 93-86343

ISBN: 0-671-89034-4

First MTV Books/Callaway/Pocket Books trade paperback printing November 1993

10 9 8 7 6 5 4 3 2

Pocket and colophon are registered trademarks of Simon & Schuster Inc.

Printed in the U.S.A.

This book is a work of fiction. Names, characters, places, and incidents
are either products of the author's imagination or are used fictitiously.

INTROSUCKTION (HUH HUH)

Like, welcome to the introsucktion, huh huh huh.

Yeah. Heh heh m heh heh.

Shut up, Beavis. Uh, do you know us?

We're like Beavis and Butt-head.

Yeah. Huh huh, we're cool. We live in this town and have crappy jobs and go to a sucky school with a bunch of morons.

We're like their leaders. And like this book is all about that crap.

I'm Butt-head. Don't get yourself too hot looking at me. I know it's hard.

This is me, Beavis. But if you're a chick you probably already know that.

Huh huh huh huh huh. I said "hard."

CAST OF CARICATCHERS

6'
5'
4'

THESE ARE LIKE SOME OF THE PEOPLE IN TOWN WHO WE ESPECIALLY LIKE TO WHALE ON.

DARIA MORGENDORFFER

THIS IS DARIA. BUT YOU CAN CALL HER DIARRHEA. GET IT? IT'S LIKE WE SCREWED UP HER NAME OR SOMETHING. SHE'S LIKE ONE OF OUR FELLOW STUDENTS. SHE REALLY RESPECTS US, 'CAUSE SHE SAID WE'RE "FREAKS OF NATURE" ONCE. WE TOLD HER NO, THAT'S VAN DRIESSEN. SHE'S REAL SMART. SHE READS LIKE MAGAZINES AND STUFF. THEY DON'T EVEN HAVE LIKE TV PEOPLE ON THE COVER.

MR. BUZZCUT

AT SCHOOL THERE'S LIKE MR. BUZZCUT. HE'S OUR HYGIENE TEACHER. I THINK HE REALLY WANTS TO TEACH WAR HYGIENE OR WAR SCIENCE OR WAR MATH. HE WAS IN SOME WAR, SEE. LIKE IN "M*A*S*H" OR WHATEVER. EXCEPT HE WASN'T A DOCTOR. HE WAS ONE OF THOSE ARMY GUYS WHO KILLS PEOPLE. YOU'D THINK THAT WOULD HAVE MADE HIM COOL.

TOM ANDERSON

WHEN WE NEED MORE MONEY THAN OUR BURGER WORLD PAYCHECK, WE GO TO THIS GUY, MR. ANDERSON. HE'S REAL OLD. HE WAS IN A WAR TOO, BUT HE'S EVEN LIKE LESS COOL THAN MR. BUZZCUT, IF THAT COULD HAPPEN. WE DO LIKE HANDYMAN STUFF FOR HIM, LIKE CHAINSAW STUFF. WHATEVER. IF HE HAD LIKE A NICKEL FOR EVERY TIME HE EATS AT BURGER WORLD, HE'D HAVE LIKE ALL THESE NICKELS.

STEWART STEVENSON

THERE ARE OTHER KIDS FROM SCHOOL, THEY'RE LIKE IN OUR PEER PRESSURE OR WHATEVER. ONE IS STEWART. HE'S LIKE THIS WUSS KID WHO'S REAL INTO "STAR TREK" AND VIDEO GAMES. HE'S GOT LIKE WHAT YOU CALL A "RELATIONSHIP" WITH HIS PARENTS. BUT HE THINKS WE'RE COOL, AND HIS PARENTS PAY FOR PAY-PER-VIEW, SO HE DOESN'T TOTALLY SUCK. NO, HE DOES TOTALLY SUCK.

MR. VAN DRIESSEN

THEN THERE'S MR. VAN DRIESSEN. HE'S A TEACHER TOO. HE TRIES TO UNDERSTAND US. ONLY IT CAN'T BE DONE, HUH HUH. HE'S LIKE THE KING OF THE HIPPIES. HE WAS AT LIKE THAT THING IN THE '60S. THAT CONCERT. FREEDOM ROCK. THE ONE WHERE JIMI HENDRIX WAS KILLED OR SOMETHING. ONE TIME HE CALLED US A "FLASHBACK." THAT WAS COOL.

OUR TOWN

Key To Our Town

1. **CITY PARK** WHERE THE COOL SENIORS AND DUDES WHO ARE TOO COOL FOR COLLEGE HANG OUT, CRANK THEIR CAR STEREOS, AND ROCK, TOTALLY KICKING TENNIS PLAYER ASS IN THE PROCESS.

2. **HIGHLAND LUMBER YARD** BEAVIS ALWAYS SAYS HE'S GOING TO BURN IT, BUT HE'S TOO LIMP TO ACTUALLY DO IT.

3. **THE UPSTAIRS DINNER THEATER** WE CALL IT "DRAMA CLUB DUDE CENTRAL." BUTT-HEAD ALMOST MADE OUT WITH A CHICK THERE, BUT SHE MUST HAVE BEEN GAY OR SOMETHING, 'CAUSE SHE SAID NO.

4. **THE SPORTS'N'WILD EXOTIC DANCING CLUB** THE ADS OUTSIDE THIS PLACE ARE REAL COOL. THERE'S A NEON DANCING CHICK IN A BIKINI. SHE HAD BIG ELECTRIC THINGIES.

5. **LARRY'S GUN RANGE COCKTAIL LOUNGE** SOMEDAY BEAVIS SAYS HE'S GOING TO KICK ASS THERE.

6. **HOME OF GOVERNMENT-PROTECTED WETLAND** YOU'RE SAFE, LITTLE FROGGIES. HUH HUH.

7. **TURBO MALL 2000** ONE TIME IN THE JEANS INTERNATIONAL DRESSING ROOM, BUTT-HEAD HOCKED A LUGEY IN THE FRONT RIGHT POCKET OF A PAIR OF 80 DOLLAR BANDINI ASS-HUGGERS ™. HUH HUH, IT WAS YELLOW AND JUICY. PET ME TAKES CREDIT CARDS, HUH HUH.

8. **THE SOUND SILO** SUCKY MUSIC STORE. THEY SELL COLLEGE MUSIC AND EVERYBODY WEARS BIG UGLY GLASSES LIKE THAT ENGLISH DUDE, ABBOT COSTELLO.

9. **BUDDY'S HOUSE OF SPORTING GOODS** THEY SELL CROSSBOWS AND 16-INCH HUNTING KNIVES. HUH HUH, YOU SAID 16 INCHES. HUH HUH. THEY SELL COOL BUMPER STICKERS, "BOWLERS HAVE BOWLING BALLS" OR SOMETHING.

10. **HOUSE WHERE BEAVIS GOT BIT BY A RABID DOG** MAN'S BEST FRIEND. THAT'S WHY IT BIT BEAVIS — HE'S NOT A MAN, HUH HUH. SHUT UP, BUTT-HEAD.

11. **MEMORIAL HOSPITAL** HUH HUH, THEY LIKE KNOW US THERE. YEAH, HEH HEH. IT'S LIKE OUR HOME AWAY FROM HOME.

12. **AQUA WORLD** DOLPHINS SUCK. HAMMERHEADS RULE.

13. **STEWART'S HOUSE** PAY PER VIEW. AND LOOK BEHIND HIS DAD'S NIGHTSTAND, HUH HUH.

14. **BURGER WORLD** HUH HUH, YOU WANT SOME FLIES WITH THAT SHAKE? HUH HUH.

15. **STARLITE DRIVE IN** SECOND-HAND CONDOM FARM. NOW PLAYING: MAN-EATING ZOMBIE CHICKS. HUH HUH, MAN EATING.

16. **HIGHLAND HIGH** AVOID AT ALL COSTS.

17. **KWIK-MART CONVENIENCE STORE** GOOD NACHOS. NACHOS KICK ASS.

18. **TOM ANDERSON'S HOUSE** JUST LOOK FOR A HOUSE WITH A BIG SIGN SPRAY PAINTED ON IT. THAT'S WHERE ANDERSON LIVES.

19. **ALMOST FLORIDA MOBILE COMMUNITY** HUH HUH. DO YOU LIKE TORNADOES? HUH HUH, YOU'LL LIKE THIS PLACE.

OUR FAMILY BUSH (HUH HUH)

26. 27. 28. 29. 30.

36.

22. 23. 41.

38. 44.

18. 17. 13. 12. 3.

14. 15. 16.

47.

19. 20. 21. 45.

46. 48.

1.

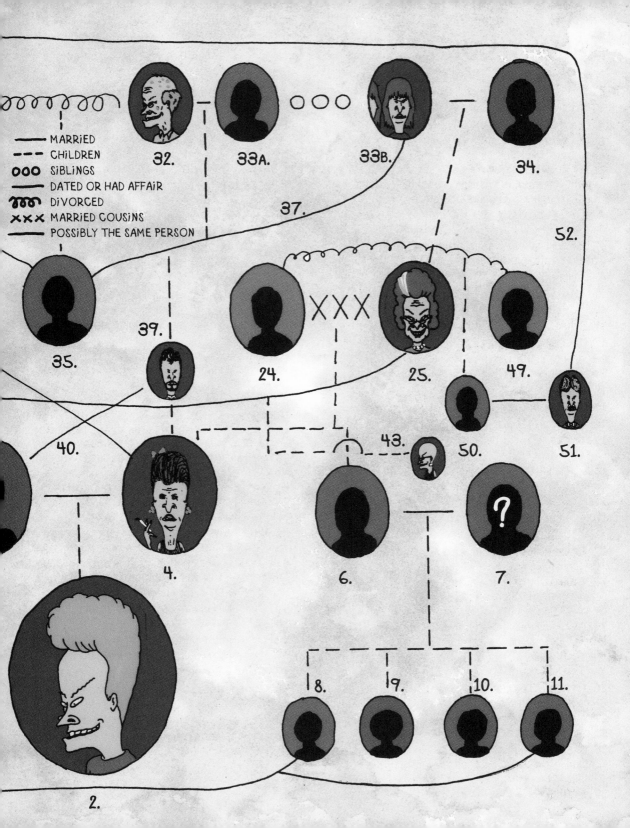

Family Bush Explained

1. Butt-head
2. Beavis
3. Butt-head's Mom
4. Beavis's Mom
5. Unknown, but could be Chester Lyle, parolee and carnival game operator; Lance Corporal Lewis Rumson, court-martialed after deserting during Grenada invasion; or Lloyd Gimler, successful nail and screw merchant. See 39
6. Aunt Cleotis, nurse at Highland County Sanatorium
7. Unknown, believed to be "Patient X," hopeless government test subject
8. Cousin Tina
9. Cousin Gina
10. Cousin Dina
11. Cousin Tina 2
12. Uncle Edgar, grocery delivery "boy"
13. Aunt Lee-Pok, former Thai madame (met Edgar during Nam)
14. Cousin Chad
15. Cousin Nguyen
16. Cousin Tiffany
17. Uncle Clyde, clerk at Juan's 24-hour Check Casheteria
18. Aunt Trish, assistant to Monsieur Troy, glass-blower-in-residence, Turbo Mall 2000
19. Cousin Norwood
20. Cousin Pearl
21. Cousin Bud
22. Grandma Butt-head, retired owner of a beauty salon for dogs
23. Grandpa Butt-head, only person in Highland County Highway Department history to be convicted of a hit-and-run with a steamroller
24. Gramps Beavis, injured back in Army, 1948, lives on pension
25. Gram Beavis, professional Bingo player, 15-card Central Southwestern Seniors' League
26. Ophelia Turner Deetz, mail-order bride from northern Saskatchewan
27. Moses Deetz, failed inventor, held patent for horse-powered car
28. Great-Grandpa Butt-head, small-time cult leader who forbade reading and washing, had three wives:
29. Esther
30. Maisie
31. and Edna, whose first marriage, to Great-Grandpa Beavis, ended in Highland County's first divorce
32. Great-Grandpa Beavis, live-animal gland remover and part-time taxidermist
33A. Lucy and her Siamese twin,
33B. Juicy
34. Wilmer Cuckold, Canadian anarchist
35. Merl Gimler, child from previous marriage of Edna and Great-Grandpa Beavis, rumored to have had affairs with...
36. Grandma Butt-head and...
37. Juicy Cuckold
38. Grandma Butt-head and Merl Gimler's illegitimate child, Chet, sent to an orphanage, believed to have joined the carnival or the Army
39. Merl and Juicy's illegitimate son, Lloyd, raised by a prominent Dallas hardware store owner
40. Beavis and Butt-head's unknown father could in fact be either Merl and Juicy's son Lloyd, or Grandma Butt-head and Merl Gimler's boy, Chet. Mrs. Beavis and Mrs. Butt-head can be sure about just one thing: the father was a man
41. Mrs. Beavis may have had affair with Grandpa Butt-head at Red Cross Crisis Center during the Tornado of '78
42. Uncle Edgar said to have delivered more than groceries to Grandma Beavis. Huh huh.
43. Grandma Beavis's secret love child, Larry Edgar. Lives in Fresno, said to do creative work in adult film business
44. Mrs. Beavis's alleged first child, Cheri. Possibly married to Chet
45. Cousin Bud divorced from Cousin Tiffany
46. Tiffany remarries Cousin Norwood
47. Cousin Bud now dating Cousin Pearl
48. Cousin Nguyen dating cousins Tina and Tina 2 simultaneously
49. Gramps Beavis's first wife, Clamonia
50. Gramps and Clamonia's daughter, Darlette
51. Mr. Troy, mall glass-blower
52. Mr. Troy had brief affair with Aunt Trish, his assistant, during 1983 glass-blowing convention in Gallup, New Mexico

Precious Moments

Age 0
This is Butt-head. HE's topless. Huh Huh.

Age 4
Cool. I can sing my ABCs as good as I could then. A-B-C, uh, Q-R-C...

Age 3 Butt-head's cousin introduces him to a frog. YEAH, and then I introduced him to my butt.

Age 4
This was like our first fishing trip. WE got lucky and caught about 60 carps. Carps taste like gunpowder.

Age 5
At Beavis's fifth birthday party, he made his wish come true.

Age 5
First day at school. The next day it started to suck.

Age 5
Beavis's first bike. That was before Mrs. Beavis said no more riding on the freeway.

Age 6
Beavis's first haircut, by Butt-head.

Age 7
Butt-head thought taking Santa hostage would be cool.

Age 8
Kwire was punishment for my first grafitti offense.
But not for long.

Age 9
Beavis played baseball 'cause he got a free bat.
Bats are cool.

Age 8
Fourth of July rules. Yeah, and getting off the critical list
on the 5th also kicks ass.

WELCOME TO THE JUNGLE

① THIS CHICK IN AN APRON AT THE MALL SAID "WANNA TRY NEW CRYSTAL SWIG?" IT TOOK LIKE TEN TRIES TO BREAK THE BOTTLE. CRYSTAL SWIG SUCKS. IT'S NOT EVEN SUGAR.

② HEY, WOULD YOU LIKE TO MEET BEAVIS'S GIRLFRIEND? HUH HUH HUH HUH.

③ WE GET CRATES OF M-80'S FROM THIS GUY IN THE PARK. HE SAID TO STOCKPILE 'CAUSE THEY'RE GONNA BE OUTLAWED. EVERY WEEK, BEAVIS WANTS TO TORCH THE BOX AND PUSH IT OUT THE WINDOW FOR FOURTH OF JULY.

④ BEAVIS SAID IT WAS THE MILLIONTH MATCH HE LIT. HE TRIED TO LIGHT A SPECIAL M-100 WITH IT, BUT I SPIT ON THE FUSE.

⑤ WE WERE GONNA DO A MIDNIGHT BOX JOB AT VAN DRIESSEN'S HOUSE, SO TO WAKE BEAVIS UP I THREW A BASEBALL AT THE WINDOW.

⑥ LOANER FROM ANDERSON. HE DOESN'T KNOW IT'S A LOANER, THOUGH. HE THINKS IT'S STOLEN. IT'S COOL TO PLAY AIR GUITAR WITH IT. UNLESS YOU TURN IT ON.

⑦ THAT'S WHERE BEAVIS KEEPS ALL HIS CLOTHES. EXCEPT FOR HIS HIGH HEELS. HUH HUH HUH HUH. THE GOVERNMENT SAYS THAT BEAVIS'S OLD CLOTHES ARE LIKE A HAZARD. YOU'LL TURN INTO BEAVIS.

⑧ ESSENTIAL FOR BOOBY TRAPS. IT'S LIKE A STEWART MAGNET. BEAVIS WANTS TO WEAR IT FOR THANKSGIVING WHEN HIS FAMILY MAKES HIM PUT ON A TIE.

⑨ WE USE THIS BAG FOR SPECIAL PROJECTS, HUH HUH. LIKE WILDLIFE RENOVATION.

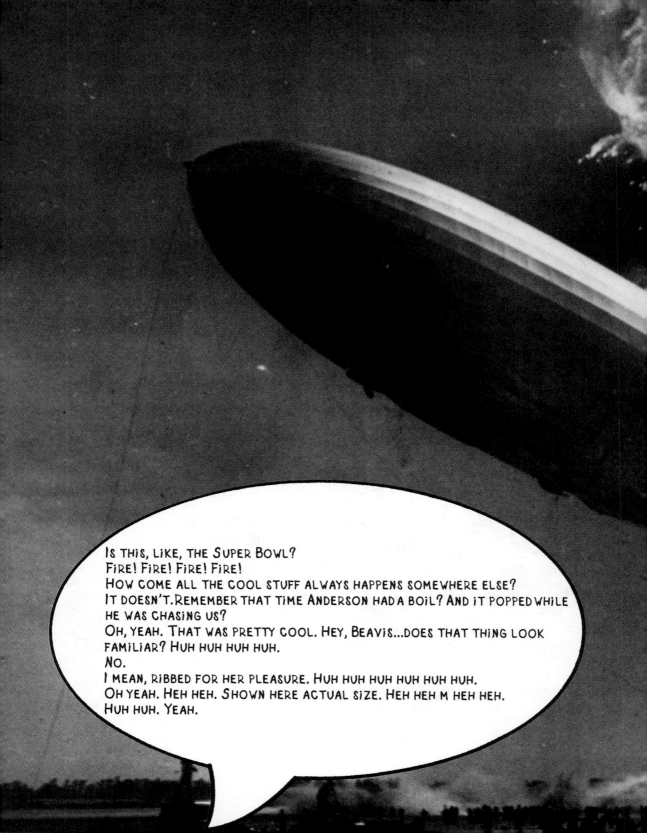

HIGHLAND HIGH
SCHOOL PSYCHIATRIST REPORT
STRICTLY CONFIDENTIAL
SUMMARY

Subjects: Beavis & Butt-head
Teacher: Buzzcut
Reporting: Dr. Floss
Indicate type of session:
X Counseling   X "Rap"   X Evaluation
X Psychotherapeutic

Reason for Referral: Subjects frequently disruptive in homeroom (especially inclined to use firecrackers). Subjects focused on excretion, sex to a degree remarkable even for age group. Subjects' pathological laughter causes severe emotional stress in those around them.

Recommendation: If I knew what to do, I might have a shot at a Nobel! Based on interviews and tests (see attached), it appears that somebody beat us to the lobotomy. Eventually, we may want to order CAT scans for possible childhood brain trauma. Personally, I suggest we discuss the possibility of graduating them early. Alternative suggestion: immediate commitment.

REPORT OF INTERVIEW
The interview went downhill from the very first moment, when Beavis gave his name as "Penis." This was followed by a long spell of the laughter I'd heard so much about.

I asked the two of them whether they felt scared about seeing the psychiatrist and they answered, I believe, characteristically. Beavis asked for electroshock therapy, and Butt-head said, "Uh, Doctor Giving Some, I presume?" This brought on another twenty or so minutes of their laughter, or so it seemed.

I believe their answers to the attached test say it all. I've cleaned it up, as their handwriting is painful to read, and attached their drawing responses to Question 5.

VOCATIONAL/DIAGNOSTIC TEST

Instructions. This is not a test. We merely want to explore how you feel in certain situations. Remember—there are no "wrong" answers, except dishonest ones.

(Note: Butt-head wrote "False" after this sentence.)

1. A mysterious man offers to take you to a desert island. What do you bring?

Butt-head: TV Guide. Kleenex.
Beavis: Matches.

2. While on your way to an important appointment, you see someone you know lying hurt in the street. What do you do?

Butt-head: Take his pants off.
Beavis: Take his wallet.
Butt-head: I already took his pants, dillweed.
Beavis: Uh, kick him? And burn his pants.

3. Talk about an important day in your life.

Butt-head: It was the day that Beavis tried to kiss me, but I kicked his ass. That's why it was an important day. 'Cause it was the first time I completely shredded Beavis.
Beavis: Shut up, bum wipe. I wasn't trying to kiss you. I tripped. Besides, I kicked your ass. But that's not important. My important day was when I kidnapped Buzzcut and brought him to my torture chamber and made him talk. I burned his pants.
Butt-head: I'm afraid that never happened, Beavis.
Beavis: No. Uh, wait. No.

4. What is your first memory?

Butt-head: Uh, I forgot. (And that laugh again.)
Beavis: Yeah. I forgot too. (Ditto.)

5. If you could be any animal in the world, which one would it be?

Butt-head: I'd be a sex animal. But I guess I am already. I guess I'd be a panther.
Beavis: Me too. Or a flying bear. That would be cool.

6. Fill-ins.

When I'm with my parents, I feel <u>myself</u>. [Butt-head]
My favorite subject in school is <u>fire</u>. [Beavis]

7. Word Associations

	Beavis	Butt-head
cat	fire	butt
white	explosion	spraypaint
God	Butthole Surfers	Butthole Surfers
apple	fire	worm
car	crash	butt

| BEAVIS: SUCKS. | BUTT-HEAD: UH, WHY DO YOU ASK? |

| BUTT-HEAD: DUDE, I'M <u>PULLING</u> MY <u>BURRITO</u>. HUH HUH HUH.
BEAVIS: HEH HEH HEH HEH. | BUTT-HEAD: BURRITOS ARE COOL. |

FREEDOEM AND WHAT HAVE I DONE TO DESerVE ITX

BUTT-head
Mr. buzzKcuts class
special Ass ignment

Freedom, and What Have I ẋ dOne to Deserve it

by Butt-head

The tittleoof1 this paper, "fFreedom,and what Have I den
ạdone to deserve it, "is a goodẋ onẉ., It is a tittle that
    4   makes you think about h what have I done to ^{de}
deserve freedom. This question oẋ oẋ of what I have done
to decerve freeẋdom is a good ẉuestion. Likke theẎ
tiẋtle. Is.

                              O
What ahve I done to ẟeserve it?/ Thatẗ isffreedom? I haẉve
sat in class a and putẋx up with people who suck. When i
wantfreedom to do things that r are cook!. kicking Beavis"s
ba ass, blewing up stẟff, watching tV ⁎ hanging out at the
   conveniense store, or the parkẋ. # That is what freedom
means to me..,

ẟre you really gona read thisẟ pape r? you Just asigned

it to geton ouẗ butt.   If you really want to read itẗ,
   then you will like it w hen I caẋll you a buttwipe
who was probably to lame tḃ join the arẉie army.I bet
  the guy frḃm r.e.M cuḃḃd could kick u your ass. Or XXXHX
even Axle.
Well
Well I see that I a,lmost out of paper. So that i is
my theme, about how ffreEdom deserves meẋ.

              The Ẻnd
                 A Butt-headẟ Pr oduction
                pRoduced and wriῗten$_{by}$ Bẏ Butt-head
              In coper ation with Butt-head Ent2erprises
                    cCopyrịt 199$_3$

INSECT COURT

CRIMINAL AND SCENE OF CRIME	CRIME	VERDICT	PUNISHMENT
THIS BEETLE WE FOUND IN THE PARK	BEING A BUG	GUILTY	DEATH BY LETHAL EXPLOSION
COCKROACH FROM THE COUCH	CHECKING OUT OUR BUTTS	GUILTY	CRUSHED IN CUSTODY
BUTTERFLY THAT LANDED ON BEAVIS'S BIKE SEAT	BIKE THEFT	GUILTY	ESCAPED; WANTED FOR ASSISTING IN THE TRASHING OF A BIKE SEAT
CENTIPEDE FROM THE STREET	TOO MANY LEGS	GUILTY	BLOWN UP; DONATED LEGS TO SCIENCE
SANDWORM FROM A VACANT LOT.	RESISTING ARREST	GUILTY	COMMUNITY SERVICE IN COUCH FISHING
DADDY LONGLEGS FROM BACKYARD	LOITERING	GUILTY	DE-LEGGED; DEATH BY MAGNIFYING GLASS
GRASSHOPPER FROM FIELD	FLYING WITHOUT A LICENSE	GUILTY	PERMANENTLY GROUNDED

GUARANTEED EFFECTIVE PICKUP LINES

51.

UH, HEY BABY.

UH, DO YOU LIKE COME HERE OFTEN, HUH HUH.
I SAID "COME."

YOU NEED A MAN IN YOUR LIFE, BABY. AND LIKE, I
NEED A WOMAN. LET'S LIKE GET INTO EACH OTHER'S
LIFE OR WHATEVER.

UH, LIKE LET'S DROP ALL THE UH B.S. AND LIKE,
YOU KNOW, DO IT.

UH, GET OUT OF MY CAR AND INTO MY DREAMS, BABY.

WHAT'S YOUR SIGN? IS IT "YIELD"? HUH HUH HUH HUH.

WOULD YOU LIKE CARRY MY BOOKS FOR ME?

IF I SAID YOU WERE SEXY, WOULD YOU HOLD YOUR
BODY AGAINST ME?

I CAN MAKE YOU FEEL LIKE I'VE NEVER
HAD SEX BEFORE.

MY LIPS ARE LIKE REGISTERED WEAPONS.

I'M NOT TRYING TO PICK YOU UP. YOU'RE LIKE TOO
HEAVY. HUH HUH HUH HUH. GET IT?

IF I WAS LIKE THE LAST MAN ON EARTH I BET WE
COULD DO IT IN PUBLIC.

IF YOU NEED A LOVE DOCTOR, I HAVE LIKE A
MEDICATED DEGREE.

IF YOU EVER HAD SEX WITH A MACHINE, THAT'S WHAT
IT'S LIKE WITH ME. 'CAUSE I'M LIKE A SEX MACHINE.

IF YOU'RE REALLY HOT, I BET I CAN COOL YOU DOWN.

HEY, ARE YOU ONE OF THOSE CHICKS WHO GOES WITH
GUYS RIGHT OFF THE BAT? 'CAUSE THAT'S WHAT I'M
LOOKING FOR.

SHOULD I CALL YOU FOR BREAKFAST OR WILL YOU
LIKE COOK IT FOR ME?

YOU MAY NOT BE REALLY HOT, BUT I BET YOU LIKE
TO DO IT.

54.

37.

ACTIVITIES SECTION

ACTIVITIES SUCK. HERE'S WHAT WE MEAN.

WORD FIND
CAN YOU FIND THE HIDDEN WORDS?

```
X  B  T  U  V  V  G  H  S  M  O  R  L  E
J  U  D  M  N  N  Q  W  Z  I  H  K  N  T
F  R  M  P  Y  L  S  T  P  M  K  C  I  M
A  G  L  H  W  S  N  O  K  A  J  L  P  W
I  R  D  E  P  K  U  B  T  U  P  L  G  H
Q  G  W  S  D  P  K  N  H  L  Z  C  E  M
X  W  V  U  I  T  S  E  K  Z  Z  Z  Z  Z
```

HINT: "NO"

CONNECT THE DOTS

24. 57. 26.

13. 43.   35. 47.

29.   34.   6. 36.   38.

59.   28.   44.

23.   2.   49. 7.   17.

1. 3. 5. 50.   14.

46. 16. 39.   31. 9.   15.

25. 4.   10.   19.   40.

8.   42.   20.

27. 33.

21.   12. 32. 18.   56.

22. 11.   60.

45.

55.   48. 41.

30.   52.

58.

LET'S COLOR!

COLORING'S PRETTY COOL, IF, LIKE, YOU HAVE A BIG ENOUGH SPACE FOR YOUR ARTISTIC VISION. WE STARTED ANDERSON'S HOUSE, BUT "DEATH TRUCK" IS ON. YOU FINISH IT.

HOW TO DRAW US

LET'S SAY YOU'RE LIKE BORED, AND
YOU WANNA DRAW ME AND BEAVIS.
THAT WOULD BE COOL.
SHUT UP, BEAVIS. OKAY, FIRST YOU
START WITH THE HEAD.
HEH HEH M HEH HEH. YOU SAID HEAD.
HUH HUH. COOL. OKAY. FOR BEAVIS,
DRAW LIKE A TRIANGLE WITH LIKE ONE
POINT GOING STRAIGHT DOWN.
THAT'S HIS HEAD. HUH HUH HUH. OH
YEAH, DRAW LIKE A CROSS IN IT.
THAT'S FOR, UH, BECAUSE, UH, JUST
DO IT AND DON'T ASK ANY QUESTIONS.
HEH HEH. BUTT-HEAD'S HEAD IS
LIKE A VOLVO.
OVAL, DUMB ASS.
HEH HEH. YEAH, OVAL. UH, PUT A
CROSS IN IT.
FOR BEAVIS'S FACE? FIRST DO HIS
HAIR. HUH HUH, IT'S LIKE MESSED UP.
BUTT-HEAD'S EYES ARE LITTLE. HEH
HEH. LIKE LITTLE BURNED UP SEEDS.
UH, MAKE BEAVIS'S TEETH MESSED UP.
BUTT-HEAD'S GOT LIKE BIG GUMS. HEH
HEH. LIKE PIECES OF RAW CHICKEN.
PUT EGGS AND CRAP ON HIS BRACES.
HE LIKES TO MUNCH.
UH, BEAVIS'S NOSE IS SORT OF LIKE,
UH, MESSED UP.
BUTT-HEAD'S NOSTRILS ARE BIG.
THEY'RE LIKE ANIMAL CAVES THAT GO
IN HIS FACE. HEH HEH.
WHEN YOU'RE DONE, THROW IT AWAY.
NO. BURN IT. HEH HEH.
HUH HUH. YEAH. BURN IT.

Instant Band Names

Combine any name from column A with any name from column B, or one from column B with one from column C, or, for maximum results, one from column A with one from column B with one from column C.

A	B	C
SATAN'S	DEATH	SHIP
FLYING	CANDY	WHEEL
BURNT	FIRE	HEAD
BLACK	CANCER	PEPPERS
STEEL	FÖKKER	MAIDEN
ATOMIC	WASTE	BASKET
POISON	MONKEY	BONER
GERMAN	FROGURT	DRUG
CHILDREN OF (THE)	LOVE	MACHINE
SCREAMING	COMA	RÝCHE
GOLDEN	CLAM	RATS
DEF	DESIRE	STICK
FATAL	WAR	SNAKE
ALBINO	MEAT	POD

ABOUT THE SAME TIME
ROMAN TIMES. ORGIES WERE COOL.

AFTER THAT
BARBARIANS TRASH ROME. COOLER.

AFTER THAT. LIKE 25, MAYBE.
THE MEDIUM AGES. DRAGONS AND SWORDS.
CHICKS WEAR THOSE THINGS AROUND
THEIR BODIES THAT SHOW OFF THEIR THINGIES.
JOAN VAN ARC BURNED AT THE STAKE.

69 A.D.
SIXTY-NINE. HUH HUH, HUH HUH.

1870
OZZY BORN.

1930
RAMBO INVENTS H-BO
AT LAS VEGAS.

1850
VIETNAM WAR. RAMBO KICKS
GERMANS' ASS.

1736
WORLD WAR III (?). AMERICA KICKS THE ENTIRE
WORLD'S ASS. MOST OF THE WORLD BLOWS UP.

1492
AMERICA KICKS ENGLAND'S ASS
IN A WAR. CIVIL WAR II.

ELEVENTY-HUNDRED
MARK POLIO INVENTS M-80s.

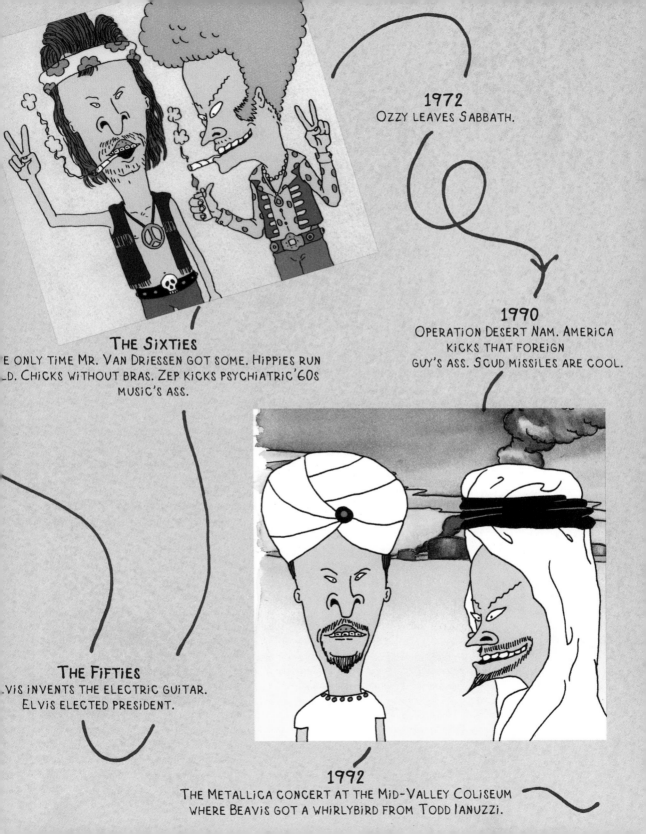

1972
OZZY LEAVES SABBATH.

THE SIXTIES
E ONLY TIME MR. VAN DRIESSEN GOT SOME. HIPPIES RUN
_D. CHICKS WITHOUT BRAS. ZEP KICKS PSYCHIATRIC '60S
MUSIC'S ASS.

1990
OPERATION DESERT NAM. AMERICA
KICKS THAT FOREIGN
GUY'S ASS. SCUD MISSILES ARE COOL.

THE FIFTIES
.VIS INVENTS THE ELECTRIC GUITAR.
ELVIS ELECTED PRESIDENT.

1992
THE METALLICA CONCERT AT THE MID-VALLEY COLISEUM
WHERE BEAVIS GOT A WHIRLYBIRD FROM TODD IANUZZI.

Dear Care Provider,

I want to share with you my feelings about your son's self-esteem problem. When a student sticks a pencil in his eye, or sets fire to the other children's homework, it's clear that he doesn't respect his own self-hood.

I've tried and tried to "stay positive," and guide your son toward a loving relationship with himself. But today, when I asked him to write a song in class, he surreptitiously inserted some sort of entrail into the sound hole of my guitar. I respect the impulse to create by challenging the rules established by society. That's what the revolution was all about. But that guitar was autographed by Pete Seeger, and it may never be completely rid of the smell.

If the behavior of your child does not change for the better immediately, I'm going to have to strongly urge that you find a healer for him. Perhaps an energy redirection therapist, or sensory deprivation chamber specialist. I would be happy to recommend some for you.

In closing, I would urge you to impress upon your son the fact that it is impolite to refer to adolescent girls' breasts as "killer thingies."

Sincerely,

David VanDriessen

P.S. Won't you please recycle this paper? The trees thank you.

 "PEACE-A-GRAM"

TATTOOS RULE!

TATTOOS KICK ASS.
MESSING UP YOUR SKIN IS
COOL. IT MAKES YOU LIKE,
EUNICH, AND TOTALLY
RELIGIONAL. THIS DUDE IN
THE PARK TOLD US THAT IN
JAPAN? THEY LIKE GIVE
THE COOLEST TATTOOS TO
THE CRIMINALS. ME AND
BEAVIS WERE GONNA HITCH
OVER THERE EXCEPT YOU
GOTTA GO TO HIGH SCHOOL
FOR LIKE 20 YEARS JUST TO
BE A CRIMINAL AND GET A
DECENT TATTOO. WE SAID
NO WAY. BUT LIKE, IF YOU
GOT A TATTOO AFTER YOU
GRADUALATED, INSTEAD OF
A DIPLOMMA, THAT WOULD
BE COOL. HIGH SCHOOL
SUCKS. THESE ARE THE
ONES ME AND BEAVIS
WOULD GET.

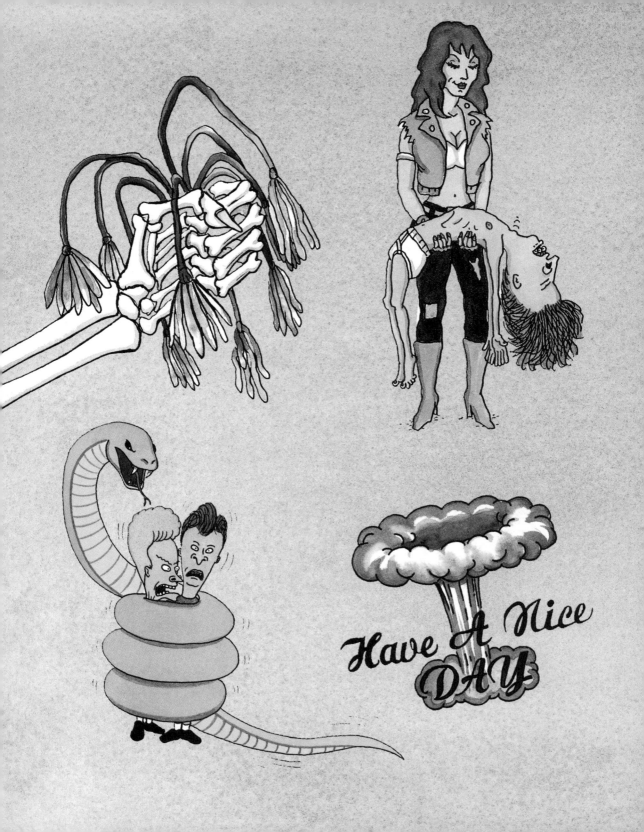

Have A Nice DAY

PROPERTY OF
GWAR

LIFE SUCKS

BURRICOS

RULE

I'M WITH STUPID

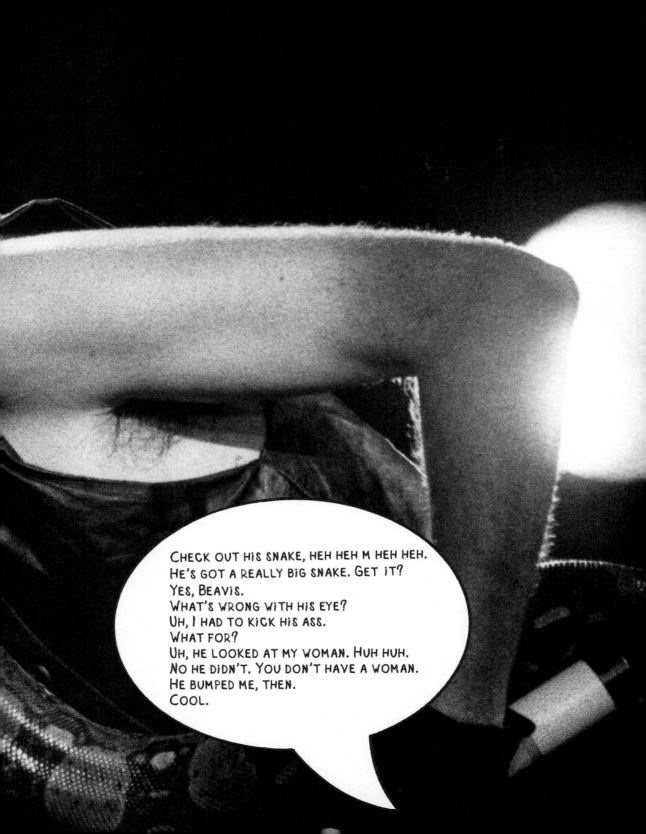

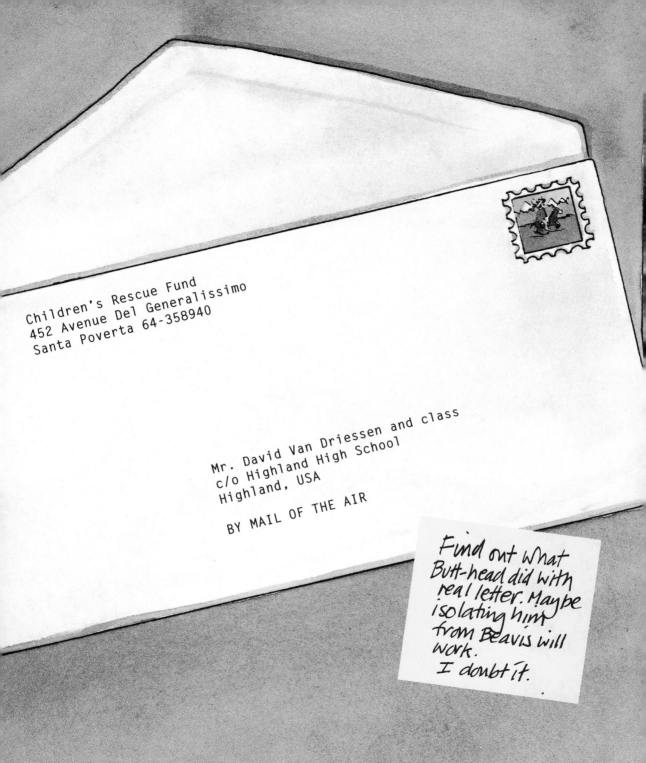

Dear Mr. Van Driessen and Class

Thank you for adopting me into your class. Here are some facks about me which you will like to know. I am 14 years old and I live in a shack with no running water or electricity. It sucks.

Here are some of our customs. Every day for breakfast we eat bats — no teachers. We like their guts best. We all have guns and we know how to use them. And the armie allows everyone to have the hand grenades, even the young people.

What is your class like? Is it run by a hippie that listens to college music? It must suck. Wurs than having no TV because you don't have electricity. I bet that your teacher has gotten senore woodrow from looking at me and my big poor eyes. He is what we call El Molester in my language and the army dudes must be called to stop him. That would be cool.

Please send me more money. Better yet, leave it behind the Burger World in a bag and I will get it myself.

Sincerely,

El Butt-head, I mean Eduardo Alicea

Free Guitar Lessons

Guitars are cool cuz they're easy to play. Hendrix burned his. He was cool. Here's the music to some kickass songs.

"The Ocean" by Led Zeppelin

DOW DOW DUNUNUNT,
DE NEH NEH, DE NEH NEH
DUN DE DUN DE
DOW DOW DUNUNUNT,
DE NEH NEH, DE NEH NEH
DUN DE DUN DE
DOW DOW DUNUNUNT,
DE NEH NEH, DE NEH NEH
DUN DE DUN DE
DOW DOW DUNUNUNT,
DE NEH NEH, DE NEH NEH
DUN DE DUN DE.

"Electric Funeral" by Black Sabbath

DAH DAH DUNT DUNT DAH-DAH
DANANANANAAH DUNT DUNT DAH-DAH.

"All Right Now" by Free

DOW, DE DUNT DUNT,
DI-DUNUH DUH-DUNUH DUN-DUNUH-DUNT
DOW, DE DUNT DUNT,
DI-DUNUH DUH-DUNUH DUH-DUNUH-DUNT.

"Ironman" by Black Sabbath

DUH NUH DUH-NUNT-DAH
DUNANUNANOW-NUNT DUH-NUNT-DAH
DUH NUH DUH-NUNT-DAH
DUNANUNANOW-NUNT DUH-NUNT-DAH.

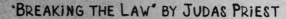

"Breaking the Law" by Judas Priest

DOW DOW DOW DE DOW DOW DE DUH-DUH
DOW DOW DOW DE DOW DOW DE DUH-DUH
DOW DOW DOW DE DOW DOW DE DUH-DUH
DOW DOW DOW DE DOW DOW DE DUH-DUH.

"Enter Sandman" by Metallica - Guitar solo
USE YOUR WAH-WAH PEDDLE FOR THIS ONE.

WHEEDLE DE WHEEDLE DE WAAAAA. WAAAAOORRR
WHOCKA WHOCKA WHEEDLE DE WHEEDLE DE
ROOOOWR WHOCKA WHOCKA
WHEEDLE DE WHEEDLE DE WAAAAA.

"Mother Russia" by Iron Maiden

DENENEH DWI NEH NEH DUNENUH
DENENEH DWI NEH NEH DUNENUT DAH
DENENEH DWI NEH NEH DUNENUH
DENENEH DWI NEH NEH DUNENUT DAH
DUNENAAH.

Special Gwar Section

"King Queen"

DUN TE-TE-TE DUNT DUNT TE-TE DUNUNUNUH
DUN TE-TE-TE DUNT DUNT TE-TE DUNUNUNUH.

"Death Pod"

DUNT DUNUNT
DUNT DUNUNUNT
DUNT DUNUNT
DUNT DUNUNUNT
DEATH POD COMES FROM THE SKY!

THAT WAS COOL.

Nuculer Nachos

- Nuculer device or like atomic particals
- Gunpowder or something
  Nacho sauce

Cover your nuculer device in the nacho sauce. Then throw the gunpowder on so it sticks. Then throw a match and run away. That would be cool.

Pudding Fun

Choklate Pudding

Go into the kichen and open the choklate puding. Put it on a pair of clean underwear. Then take the underwear back to the couch and eat the puding in front of Beavis. You should bet Beavis 10 dolers before that you'll do this.

Cooking Is Cool

EASY OMELET

1 DOSEN EGGS

TAKE EGGS AND CARRY THEM ON YOUR BIKE. THROW THEM AT WINDOWS. ALLOW 30 SECONDS FOR REACTION. GET THE HELL OUT OF THERE.

CHOKLATE GOLF BALL FAKEOUT A LA STEWART

1 DOZEN GOLF BALLS ("BALLS," HUH HUH)
CHOKLATE SYRUP

WHEN STEWART WON'T LET YOU IN THE HOUSE CAUSE HIS PARRENTS ARE AWAY, DO THIS: COVER THE GOLF BALLS WITH CHOKLATE. YOU ONLY HAVE TO DO THE TOPS, ASSMUNCH—HE'S NOT GONNA REALY EAT 'EM. TELL STEWART YOU HAVE A LIKE PREZENT FOR HIM, THESE CHOKLATE GOLF BALLS. THEN WHEN HE LET'S YOU IN, MAKE HIM EAT THEM. THEN, WHEN HE CRIES, TELL HIM HOW HE'S IN THE CLUB AND NOW YOU CAN WATCH PAY-PER-VIEW. YOU CAN USE BROWN CRAYON FOR THE CHOKLATE.

CHEN HINTS

- HE BEST WAY TO EAT COOKIES IS LIKE TRAIGHT OUT OF THE TUBE BEFORE YOU COOK THEM.

- "CREAM-FILLED SNACK CAKES" IS FUNNY.

- ALWAYS COOK AT THE HIGHEST TEMPERATURE 'CAUSE IF LIKE BEAVIS HAS PUT A BUG IN IT YOU HAVE TO LIKE KILL IT.

- DON'T PICK UP A SMOKING POT WITH YOUR BARE HANDS. MAKE BEAVIS DO IT.

- NACHOS RULE.

BUTT-HEAD: TV SUCKS. THERE'S NOTHING GOOD ON NOW.
BEAVIS: SO WHAT ARE WE GONNA DO?

BUTT-HEAD: GO GET THE DICTIONARY. WE'LL LOOK UP DIRTY WORD
BEAVIS: I DON'T WANNA GET IT. YOU GET

BEAVIS: LET'S GET SOME NACHOS, DUDE!

BUTT-HEAD: BUTTMUNCH!
BEAVIS: ASSWIPE!

BEAVIS: HEH HEH. YOU SAID "DIC."

CRITICS' CHOICE
LiKE, iF WE RAN TV.

11:35 ② DICK CLARK'S "SORRY BOSS!"★★ 23862
Re-enactments and actual footage of some of America's funniest workplace goofs, foul-ups, and disfiguring industrial mishaps.

2:45 ⑤ ACTS OF GOD★★ 12346
A bikini-clad Heather Locklear learns firsthand about some of the most gruesome accidents, assaults, and break-ins insurance claims adjusters have gotten out of paying for.

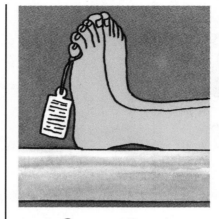

8:30 ⑪ I, CORONER★ 23912
Educational PBS docu-mystery lets you practice your knowledge of forensic medicine with a new, unidentified corpse each week.

12:30 ② CATFISH HUNTER'S FISH IN A BARREL★ 21114
It's the best of both worlds when Hall-of-Famer Catfish Hunter introduces Mickey Mantle, John Goodman, and Wink Martindale to the exciting sport of fishing with guns.

1:30 ④ FRED GRANDY'S HOW GOOD CAN YOU SWIM?★★ 23611
Game show hosted by Iowa Congressman and former TV star Fred Grandy in which contestants must complete increasingly difficult swimming challenges and underwater escapes to win cash prizes.

2:30 ⑪ MEXICAN COCKFIGHTING★
Hosted by Ricardo Montalban and Jim Lampley.

1:30 ⓐ DEATH TRUCK★★★★
Story of a top-secret government plan to put artificial intelligence in an 18-wheeler. Thirteen stuntmen killed in the making. **Violence and adult language.**

6:30 ⑪ CELEBRITY ROULETTE★★★
Five celebrities test their nerve and revitalize their careers in an actual game of Russian Roulette. Week one: Richard Thomas, Lance Kerwin, Bruce Boxleitner, Valerie Harper, and Jane Wiedlin.

Words

Weird Al "Yank"ovic
Dictate
Suckling
Salt Peter
Half Cocked
Abreast
Fluctuate
Peninsula
Penal code
Unisex Hair
Softballs
Rubber
Gas
Virgin
Virgo
Virginia
West Virginia
Sack
Plow
Eat
Boob Tube
Gland
Hard
Harden
Hardly
Anfernee Hardaway
Stiff
Wood

Intercourse
Discourse
Golf course
Of course
Escrow
Sexagenarian
Wean
Staph infection
Tungsten
French Vanilla
Public
Titillate
Sirloing
Abut
Crackle
Reared
Pole vault
Remember
Uranus
Liquor
Cockpit
Sacrifice
Creamed
Dichotomy
Can't
Pistol
Pestle
Pistil

Cock-a-doodle-doo
Charles Dickens
Dick Gregory
Little Richard
Clean and Jerk
Choke
Clutch
Squeezably Soft
Nibble
Ribs
Lance
Sock
Boing
Munch
Eat
Pump
Bone
Poke
Nail
Hammer
Finger
Peterbilt
Flog
Direct
Homogenized
Blue
Bum
Sack

Tom Anderson's True Tales of War

These're my medals from the big one, double-ya double-ya two. Back then, it was different from now. You respected your country and you believed in hard work. There weren't so many kids back then, either. It was a real good war. Always a lot of crazy stunts and practical jokes to fill the time.

1. This one's from boot camp. Why, I woke up every morning at 2 to shine my buttons, polish my boots, clean my gun, and swab the latrine. Then I got rode all day by my sergeant. At night, the other guys elected me to clean their equipment, too, so I usually didn't get to sleep before 3.

2. Pearl Harbor. Oh, sure, I was there. Marine detachment watching the ships. The fellas had a vote and I was real honored when they picked me to row into the harbor to draw enemy fire. Those guys were the greatest. I felt for them when the barracks was bombed by mistake while I was in the Harbor.

3. Guadalcanal. We was pinned down by a Japanese machine gun nest and some of the guys suggested I should bring some sandwiches to the Japs 'cause they was probably hungry. I guess I startled them 'cause they surrendered when I got to the nest. Heck, after a few days of C rations, I felt like surrendering too!

4. This one's from 1943 in Sicily. Beautiful people, them Italianos. My sarge dared me to go ring the doorbell of a man by the name of Dan Corleone and then run away. Well, he caught me, but then he laughs and kisses me on both cheeks! Next thing you know, I get this medal. I guess he had some friends back in the States in government or something.

5. Anzio, '44. My Purple Heart for getting shot in the head. The doctor told me the bullet had buried itself about 4 or 5 inches from my brain. Too close for comfort, if you ask me. The funny thing was that he said the bullet was American. I guess the Krauts had got ahold of some of our ammo somehow, the bastards. Good thing I wasn't hurt.

6. You ever see "The Longest Day" with John Wayne? Well, that was Operation Overlord, a.k.a. D day. I was there. Couple a Frogs I got friendly with gave me directions to a real good French toast place, but I musta got mixed up 'cause I got caught smack dab in the middle of a panzer division. I ran and they chased me right into a ditch and busted up their tanks. I'd like to go back and find that French toast place some day.

7. Battle of the Bulge. The Germans was firing their new rockets at us for days. My C.O. told me the rockets were really Martians coming to help the Americans win the war and would I go out and open up an unexploded rocket and say hi. Well, I did, and I accidentally defused the thing, which was good 'cause I saved a bunch of nuns who was just walking past.

8. Berlin 1945. The fellas all told me they were going to a bar and I should meet them at some place called "The Bunker." Well, you know me and directions. I got to a bunker but it was owned by Mr. Adolf Hitler, but I didn't know that 'til I tried to order a beer. He had a headache and he needed to go take some pills and lie down. Next thing you know, the place is on fire. I thought for sure I'd get blamed, but I got this medal instead.

Inside Beavis's Pocket

Van Driessen showed us how to use this for like cience. Grasshoppers and ants don't like cience, huh huh.

This guy told Beavis it's some kind a Fil Lapeeno Army knife. He can't open it. You got to be strong in Fil Lapeeno.

Beavis has had this note from school since 1988. Pretty good.

Stewart gave his key to us when we said we'd be his friends all afternoon.

The guy in the store told Beavis it was in Nam. It's broke. It sucks.

Chicks like it when you show you know sex.

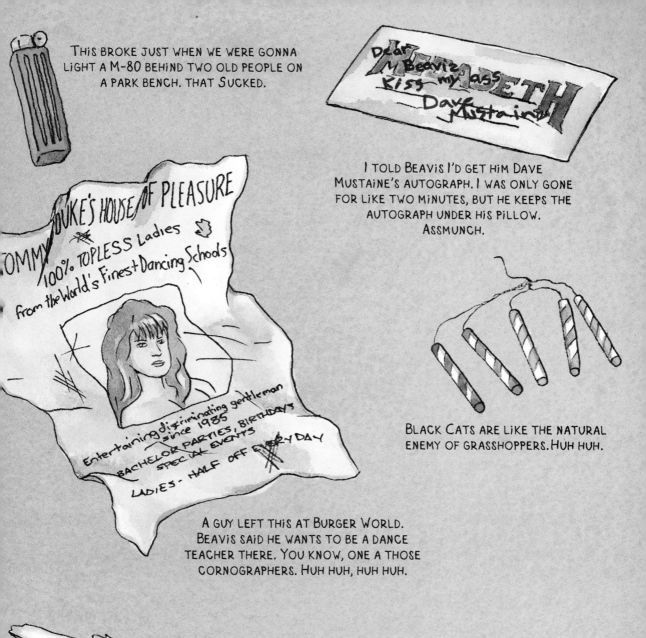

THIS BROKE JUST WHEN WE WERE GONNA LIGHT A M-80 BEHIND TWO OLD PEOPLE ON A PARK BENCH. THAT SUCKED.

Dear M Beavis
MACBETH
Kiss my ass
—Dave Mustaine

I TOLD BEAVIS I'D GET HIM DAVE MUSTAINE'S AUTOGRAPH. I WAS ONLY GONE FOR LIKE TWO MINUTES, BUT HE KEEPS THE AUTOGRAPH UNDER HIS PILLOW. ASSMUNCH.

TOMMY DUKE'S HOUSE OF PLEASURE
100% TOPLESS Ladies
from the World's Finest Dancing Schools
Entertaining discriminating gentleman since 1985
BACHELOR PARTIES, BIRTHDAYS SPECIAL EVENTS
LADIES - HALF OFF EVERY DAY

A GUY LEFT THIS AT BURGER WORLD. BEAVIS SAID HE WANTS TO BE A DANCE TEACHER THERE. YOU KNOW, ONE A THOSE CORNOGRAPHERS. HUH HUH, HUH HUH.

BLACK CATS ARE LIKE THE NATURAL ENEMY OF GRASSHOPPERS. HUH HUH.

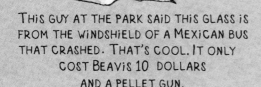

THIS GUY AT THE PARK SAID THIS GLASS IS FROM THE WINDSHIELD OF A MEXICAN BUS THAT CRASHED. THAT'S COOL. IT ONLY COST BEAVIS 10 DOLLARS AND A PELLET GUN.

HIGHLAND HIGH

OFFICIAL SCHOOL DISPATCH
Command Outpost: Highland High,
Department of Hygiene
12 November 1993
0800
Regarding: Extreme Disciplinary Breakdown of Students
Beavis and Butt-head

Parent or Current Occupant:

A discipline condition has been ongoing re: Beavis and
Butt-head dating from 9 September 1993. This condition is
characterized by chronic actions of gross insubordination
such as the following selected incidents:

Incident: Partial immolation of Beavis's work station.
Cause: Disposable butane incendiary device. 9-9-93

Incident: Random bursts of individual condiment packets—
mustard, ketchup—throughout hallway, classroom sectors.
17 bystanders sprayed. 9-15-93

Incident: Distribution of hair-removing chemicals
throughout street clothes of student Stewart Stevenson
during mandatory gym class. Student now requires
counseling 3 days per week. 9-30-93

Incident: Electrical fire in biology lab. Cause:
extension cord attached to instruction aid (pig fetus)
and plugged into socket. Result: fetus cooked, partially
eaten; substantial smoke and water damage to 6 biology
work stations. 10-7-93

Incident: Numbers "666" and name "Seymour Butts"
repeatedly scratched into wall of 2nd-floor west wing
boys' bathroom right-hand stall. Beavis apprehended by
janitor, but claims to have been incapacitated by
"fumes." 10-19-93

Incident: Student Daria Morgendorffer reports notebooks
missing. Partially charred pages of said notebooks
observed floating across athletic fields after small
explosions heard on roof. Despite holding several pages
of Human Sexuality notes with marginal doodles of
Morgendorffer practicing signature, Butt-head issues
total denial. 10-29-93

Incident: 30 children leave school sick. Cause:
contamination of water supply by gasoline, small
explosives (M-80s), and bodily fluids genetically traced
to Beavis and Butt-head. 11-8-93

Incident: School performance of "Charley's Aunt"
disrupted when two hooded individuals wearing nothing
but socks over their genitals prance on stage screaming
"Breaking the law, breaking the law." Beavis later
apprehended after it is noticed his pants are on
backwards. 11-11-93

Recommendations: Barring neutralization with Extreme
Prejudice, this teacher recommends corporal punishment,
i.e., flogging, solitary confinement, and hard labor
detail. Teacher also recommends thorough psychiatric
evaluation of students, and treatment on an ongoing
basis. We advise you to take firm and decisive action
soonest.

Please acknowledge receipt of dispatch by signature, and
return to Department of Hygiene, Highland High, 11-15 or
at earliest convenience.

Bradley Buzzcut, B.S., M.A.
Group Leader, Department of Hygiene
Highland High

From the Mail Box

I THINK YOU TWO ARE DOING THE WORK OF
BEELZEBUB. —L.N., COVINGTON, KY

BUTT-HEAD: UH, THAT'S NOT A QUESTION.
BEAVIS: WHO?
BUTT-HEAD: I THINK THAT'S, LIKE, THE DEVIL'S LAST
NAME.
BEAVIS: SHE SAID WE WERE DOING THE WORK OF
THE DEVIL?
BUTT-HEAD: I WISH THE DEVIL WOULD GIMME SOME
MONEY THEN.
BEAVIS: YEAH. HE SHOULD BUY US STUFF.

I'M IN SCHOOL AND I JUST CAN'T SEEM TO HANG
WITH THE COOL KIDS. ANY SUGGESTIONS?
—J.J., WALLINGFORD, CT

BUTT-HEAD: UH, I GOT A SUGGESTION. GET PAY-
PER-VIEW AND SOME FOOD. THEN PAY US 8 DOLERS
EACH AND YOU CAN HANG OUT WITH US FOR
PRACTICE.

WHO'S SMARTER? —G.Y., MENLO PARK, CA

BEAVIS: BUTT-HEAD'S A BRAIN. I SAW HIM READING A
ARTICLE IN A PLAYBOY.
BUTT-HEAD: BEAVIS IS SMARTER 'CAUSE HE HANGS
OUT WITH ME. I'M STRONGER 'CAUSE I KICK HIS ASS.
BEAVIS: HERE'S A BRAIN TEST. WHAT DOES A
MORON SAY?
BUTT-HEAD: WHAT?
BEAVIS: I DON'T KNOW.
BUTT-HEAD: YOU'RE NOT SO SMART AFTER ALL.

WHAT DO YOU WANT TO BE WHEN YOU GROW UP?
—M.S., DALLAS, TX

BEAVIS: I'M GONNA BE A MARINE SO I CAN KICK ASS.
PLUS PEOPLE HAVE TO SALUTE YOU.
BUTT-HEAD: HUH HUH, BEAVIS JUST WANTS TO
STAND AT ATTENTION.
BEAVIS: BUTT-HEAD WANTS TO BE A CAMPER 'CAUSE
HE LIKES PITCHING HIS TENT.
BUTT-HEAD: HUH HUH. YEAH. THAT'S PRETTY FUNNY,
BEAVIS.
BEAVIS: A FIREMAN WOULD BE COOL TOO.

WHERE ARE YOUR MOMS? —B.R., PANAMA CITY, FL

BUTT-HEAD: BEAVIS'S MOM IS PROBABLY WITH YOU.
HUH HUH HUH.
BEAVIS: SHUT UP, BUTT-HEAD. HEH HEH HEH.

WHAT'S YOUR FAVORITE SUBJECT IN SCHOOL?
—D.A., PROVO, UT

BEAVIS: SEX EDUCATION, HEH HEH M HEH HEH.
BUTT-HEAD: BEAVIS, I DON'T BELIEVE THEY TEACH
SEX EDUCATION IN OUR SCHOOL.
BEAVIS: RIGHT. COMMANDO TACTICS!
BUTT-HEAD: THEY DON'T TEACH THAT EITHER. MY
FAVORITE IS FOOD FIGHTS.
BEAVIS: I LIKE GOING TO THE NURSE. SHE SAYS I'M A
PSYCHOSOMANIC. THAT'S COOL.
BUTT-HEAD: SCHOOL SUCKS.

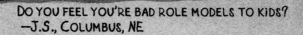

DO YOU FEEL YOU'RE BAD ROLE MODELS TO KIDS?
—J.S., COLUMBUS, NE

BUTT-HEAD: SHE SAID "MODEL."
BEAVIS: DOES SHE WANT TO SEE US IN OUR
SWIMSUITS?
BUTT-HEAD: I THINK SHE WANTS US TO BE A EXAMPLE.
BEAVIS: LIKE ON THOSE COMMERCIALS FOR DRUGS?
BUTT-HEAD: YEAH. IF YOU TAKE DRUGS YOU CAN'T
EAT EGGS. SO DON'T TAKE DRUGS.

TEEN LEGENDS OF HIGHLAND HIGH: AN ORAL HISTORY
By Daria Morgendorffer
Human Sciences/Extra Credit Project
October 15

It is said that the windows into a group's cultural behavior and development are its myths and legends. For my extra credit essay, I asked two Highland students to share with me some of the myths and legends that surround their group: the Highland High community. The following is an excerpt from my interview:

DM: What are some of the legends of Highland High?
Butt-head: That Beavis likes girls, huh huh.
Beavis: Heh heh. Shut up assmunch. She means like that one dude.
Butt-head: Oh yeah, like that dude. He was, uh, what you call a uh...
Beavis: Like a person who goes to school here...
DM: A student?
Butt-head: Yeah. He was like a student. And him and this girl were in his car, and they were, uh, you know, doing it, huh huh.

Beavis: Yeah, heh heh, they were engaged in sexual inter-state, heh heh.

Butt-head: Yeah, and then this other dude came and killed them.

DM: Another student?

Butt-head: No. He was a psycho guy who had escaped. Like Ozzy, except without his band. It was like on the radio that he had escaped. And he was psycho.

Beavis: Yeah, Ozzy killed this dude and the chick in the car because he was psycho.

DM: And they had heard the report?

Beavis: What report?

DM: The couple had heard the report on the radio but chose to ignore the warnings and decided to go ahead with their tryst and, as a consequence, paid with their lives?

Butt-head: Is that what happened?

DM: I don't know. I'm asking you.

Beavis: I thought you were supposed to have a high, uh, uh...

DM: IQ?

Beavis: What's that?

Butt-head: Huh huh. It's something only girls have, huh huh.

Beavis: Heh heh, yeah. Heh heh. I saw my mom's IQ once.

Butt-head: I bet your dad never did.

Beavis: Shut up, Butt-head.

DM: Getting back to the legend. Would you say that it's a cautionary tale meant to scare other students from engaging in illicit sex?

Beavis: She said "sex". Heh heh.

Butt-head: Yeah. Uh, this legend means not to have illegal sex with the radio on. Huh huh.

Beavis: Yeah, 'cause Ozzy will kill you. Heh heh.

Butt-head: Cool.

Hi Koo

This video sucks
Yeah, it needs more explosions
Yeah, Bonnie Raitt sucks.

Dude, check out that chick
Huh huh, she's checking me out
She's hot for my love.

Give us your homework
And we promise we won't call
You Diarrhea.

Whoa, stock car racing
Out-of-control spinouts and flame
Huh huh, we're there, dude.

It's cool not to suck.
'Cause I don't like stuff that suck
I like stuff that's cool.

If I won Lotto
I would just buy the school and
Completely trash it.

This morning was cool
There was a huge thunderstorm
Then we blew up terds.

For Christmas morning
It would be cool if I got
A submachine gun.

This lighter is broke
When i flick it it just sparks
Heh, this lighter sucks.

IT WOULD BE COOL IF
SCHOOL WERE CANCELLED OR SOMETHING
BET IT WON'T HAPPEN.

THERE WAS THIS SHOW ONCE
THIS GUY LIKE LIVED WITH TWO CHICKS
I BET THEY DID IT.

BEAVIS FRIED A MOUSE
AND SERVED IT TO ANDERSON
AT BURGER WORLD, DUDE.

HEH HEH M HEH HEH
BUTT-HEAD CRACKED A BIG STIFFY
LOOKING AT "BAYWATCH."

BURNING CHERRY TREE
EVERY BLOSSOM WAS AFLAME
UH, HERE COME THE COPS.

HEH HEH M HEH HEH
BUTT-HEAD, THAT CHICK LOOKED AT ME
HEH HEH M HEH HEH.

W Burger World W

Welcome to ~~Burger~~ World

Thank you for choosing this Burger World restaurant! Our goal is to give you the "three Fs": ~~Fresh, Friendly, and Fast.~~

Because we know that you—like all of our over 400 *billion* Burger World customers—are "special."

Our ~~People~~ Make the Difference

A smiling, friendly face taking your order. A polite "thank you" at the drive-thru. You can expect the most from every Burger World employee. Because every Burger World employee has been highly trained to meet your needs in the friendliest, most you-orientated way possible.

application with your order? There's no better way to enjoy while you ~~learn.~~

And by the way—if *you'd* like to get in on the friendly fun of being a Burger World employee, and are under 21 or ~~over 65,~~ why don't you ask for an

Get to Know Our ~~Food~~ Ass

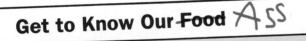

wouldn't be at a Burger
rld if you didn't know
at quality tastes like. But
u may not have known
at our hamburgers are
w made *entirely* of beef.
that every fish species
ed in our Somethin' Fishy
ndwich can be found right
re in America. Or that
en you order a Hot Cow
uit Flavor Pie, you can bet
u're getting something
at lives up to its name.

And remember, all of our
Burger World food is
cooked right here, at the
actual restaurant you're
visiting. That's a promise to
you.

A Quality ~~Dining~~ Experience Munching

clean, bright place where
u can eat your meal.
u've come to expect it
om a restaurant. So we've
t cleanliness goals for
very Burger World
staurant that even exceed
ost local health
epartments'! And chances
re you'll never feel
rammed into your seat,
cause they're extra-wide.
o bring your healthy
appetite and enjoy! Die

Dear Santa Claus

When you get like crap in your beerd, do you clean it with a Santary Napkin? That's funny. If you havg a heart attack, who gets your elves? Could we have them? It would be for sience. Just put it in your will.

Get us this Christmas:

A bunch of M-100s
Flamthrowsr
A Harley
Chicks. Real ones.
Throing stars
Torturg stuff (like what we stoll from Buzzcut)
Rat meat for Burger World
Speers
Faces of Death Video. One thru VEE.
If thsy make a cherry atomic bomb, we want that to
75 dolers for expenses

We were good this year. Beavis was gonna torch the lumber yard but he's a wuss.

Sinserely,
Beavis and Butt-head

It's another ELF-It!

These are the guys. Refer to Big Boss.

Santa Claus Headquarters

TO: Beavis & Butt-head
FR: Santa Claus
DATE: December 15, 1993

Dear Boys,
It isn't often I reply personally to one of my
letters. But you and I know each other very well,
as I'm sure you're aware.

Let me refresh your memory:

1988 Bear trap left down Butt-head's chimney.

1989 Glue traps left for reindeer on Beavis's roof.

1990 Unidentified slime left in Butt-head's stocking
for me to find.

1991 Plate of cookies covered with milky substance
that turns out to be definitely *not* milk.

1992 Request list includes the heads of entire faculty
of Highland High.

With this record, I feel I cannot grant any of
your wishes. May I also add that I know if you've been
bad or good and, consequently, I hope you
go to hell.

Merry Christmas,

Santa Claus

NORTH POLE MEMORANDUM

One-time-only Limited Collector's Edition!
The Songs of David Van Driessen!

Women Are Better Than Men

Strength and beauty, love and power
These are the petals of a woman-flower
Nourish our souls with your female milk
Velvet kisses soft as silk

Women are better than men
They are the earth and we are the moon
We are the knife and they are the spoon
Yes, women are better than men

Ancient knowledge wrapped in suede
She is your mother and not your maid
We rape their nostrils with our musky scent
Cleanse our souls with punishment

Women are better than men
We are the lion and they are the tamer
They are the artist and we are the maimer
Yes, women are better than men

Men are lazy, filthy and crude
Our objective is to search for food
We can't be trusted with our neighbor's wife
I will hate myself for the rest of my life

Women are better than men
We are the rocks and they are the soil
They are the otter and we are the oil
Yes, women are better than men.

I Heard the Beavers Screaming

I heard the beavers screaming
I heard the butterflies cry
I heard the trees a-dreaming
Of moving to the sky

I heard the toucans sobbing
I heard the wallabees wail
I felt the forest throbbing
With the shrieking of the snails

Chorus

People, people, people, people,
People can't you see
The earth's the place where nature lives
Let's love her tenderly

I heard the mountains bawling
I heard the horses bleat
I heard the woodchucks calling
To the swallows in the street

All the creatures of the canyon
All the creatures of the sea
For all the hell we've caused them
They won't be friends with me.

Chorus

The Ballad of Beavis and Butt-head

I've taught for many and many a year
Seen students come and go
Some kids can learn at the speed of light
And some are kind of slow

But there was no kid I couldn't reach
No heart I couldn't touch
Till Beavis and Butt-head came along
And had my skills for lunch

They look like they're lead singers
In some unholy choir
They'll shoot their BBs, trash their desks
And set your beard on fire

And through it all they'll laugh and laugh
Like some Satanic tape
I hear it in my sleep at night
Huh huh-there's no escape

And when I tried to reach them
And tried to understand
They took their fingers from their noses
And wiped them in my hand

And when the school year ended
When the destruction was done
They asked me to pull their fingers
And said that they'd had fun

So when I see them walking
Down my school's once-hallowed hall
I contemplate a new career
Selling menswear in a mall.

Chopping Wood with My Father

My father never liked me much
He said that I was weak
He cursed my glasses and my hair
He called me hippy freak

For years I tried to win his love
Through poetry and song
Then Alzheimer's destroyed his mind
And he won't last for long

Chorus

Chopping wood with my father
Raise the axe blade high
The old man doesn't know my name
And soon he's gonna die, boys,
Yes, soon he's gonna die

My brother Tom was strong and fast
A Special Forces star
Dad punched me out the day Tom died
On a mission in Qatar

And still I tried to please him
I washed his Cadillac
But the only time that we were close
Was chopping wood out back.

Chorus

Dear Ozzy

Me and Beavis are riting cuz we wanted to
tell you something. Your Music Kicks ass. How old
are you? You kick ass for being as old as you are.
This dude said you ate a live chicken one time.
Beavis put a frog in his mouth once. No buzz,
though. Dont eat at Burger World cuz it's not all
Meat. You know how you have your name
tatood on you'rg fingers. That's cool. Beavis was
going to get his name tatood but not on his
fingers. It wouldnt fit, though. Ok Beavis wants
to talk now.

SUCKS

Butt-head sucks

Ok Im back. Beavis is like Messed up. Can you
send us some money. like 400 dolers. And a gitar.
could we borow a miget? what do they Eat?
were in school now. You probly hard of it.
Highland High. It sucks. like here's a question.
when do you ever use English once you get
out of school? See how Messed up it is. Its like
all this totaly usless crap. Ok dude thats all
for now. Send us the mony right away. Dont
Eat any frogs dude. Can we get some tikets?

FIRE!

COOL

Butt-head Beavis

PARTY JOKES

THIS GUY WALKS INTO A BAR? AND HE SAYS, "I GOT LIKE A DOG THAT TALKS." SO THE BARTENDER SAYS, "LET'S SEE IT." AND THE GUY GOES, "I GOT IT RIGHT HERE."

SO THEN THE BARTENDER GOES TO THE DOG, "HERE'S A TEN. GO AND GET ME A BEER." AND THE DOG GOES, "YOU DO IT BUTTHOLE." HUH HUH HUH HUH.

OK, SO THEN THE DOG GOES OUT. AND THEN HE GOES INTO THIS ALLEY AND GIVES A GIRL DOG $10. AND THEN THEY DO IT DOGGIE STYLE. 'CAUSE SEE, HE NEVER HAD THE MONEY BEFORE. OK, SO THEN IT'S GETTING LATE AND LIKE THE OWNER'S TOTALLY BUZZED SO HE COMES OUT LOOKING FOR THE DOG. AND THEN HE SEES THE DOG AND HE'S LIKE, HUH HUH, STUCK TO THE OTHER ONE. SO HE LIKE SPRAYS WATER AND BEATS THE DOG TO UNSTICK IT. IT HAD LIKE A DOG BONER. HUH HUH.

OUR UNERECTED DICTIONARY SAYS THAT "BEAVIS" IS ANOTHER WORD FOR ASSWIPE.

I'D RATHER HAVE LIKE A BOTTLE IN FRONT OF ME THAN A FRONT OF A BOTTLE. HUH HUH.

HOW DO YOU KNOW WHEN A DOG IS SLEEPING WITH YOUR WIFE? 'CAUSE YOU LIKE FIND HIM IN BED WITH HER, SLEEPING.

A HAM SANDWICH WALKS INTO A BAR AND GOES, "DO YOU SERVE FOOD HERE?" AND THE BARTENDER GOES, "NO."

THIS DUDE IS TALKING TO THIS OTHER DUDE AND HE GOES, "MY WIFE THINKS SHE'S LIKE A CHICKEN."

AND THE OTHER DUDE GOES, "WHY DON'T YOU TAKE HER TO THE PSYCHOTICIST?" AND LIKE THE OTHER DUDE GOES, 'CAUSE LIKE I NEED SOME MILK." HUH HUH HUH HUH.

SO THIS SALESMAN'S CAR BREAKS DOWN IN FRONT OF A FARMHOUSE. HE SOLD CONDOMS, HUH HUH HUH HUH. AND HE GOES TO THE FARMER, "CAN I SLEEP HERE TONIGHT?" AND THE FARMER GOES, "I GOT A SPARE BED NEXT TO MY DAUGHTER, BUT IF YOU DO HER, I'LL KILL YOU."

SO THEN, IN THE MIDDLE OF THE NIGHT, THE FARMER STARTS TO DO IT WITH THE GUY ANYWAY. BUT THEN THE NEXT DAY THE FARMER GOES, "DID YOU DO IT WITH MY DAUGHTER?" AND THE GUY GOES, "NO. DID YOU?" AND THE GUY WAS A CONDOM SALESMAN. PLUS THE FARMER HAD SOME CHICKENS, AND ONE OF THEM GOES, "NOBODY HERE BUT US CHICKENS." HUH HUH. THAT HAPPENED LIKE THE NEXT DAY OR SOMETHING. IT WAS COOL.

Dear Journal,

Did you ever think that no one likes you? I guess you couldn't, you're a journal! But I do.

I used to think that Beavis and Butt-head were cool but now I guess their really just jerks. After I got my lawn darts for Children's Day (Dad just "made up" Children's Day! I love my Dad!) they came over. We had fun throwing them at each other and getting out of the way. But then they threw one at Sean O'Canine and hit him! He howled and howled and then they threw another one and ran away. And he's over 70 in people years!

When they came back they were mad 'cause Dad had took the darts. Beavis tried to light our lawn nome and Butt-head said there was no reason to stay if all the cool stuff was gone. I said would it be better if I just gave them money so they could buy they're own stuff and Butt-head said no but he took $5 and said he would think about it.

Now I guess I think of everything in a whole different light. Like when they said Monday that the Indians used wedgies to see how brave a person was, but now I think they said that so I would go ok give me a wedgie which I did. I was gonna show them my new game Boy cartridges tomorrow but no way. Stewart

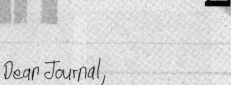

Dear Journal,

Good news! Beavis and Butt-head and I friends again! The three Amigos are back and ready to kick butt! I knew they probably were acting mean 'cause they were worried about Sean O'Lanine, but the vet says he'll probably be OK as long as we change the bag every 4 hours and keep the wound moist with ointment and mash up his food. Isn't that great? I guess you can't answer. I keep forgetting.

What happened was I brought Game Boy to school anyway 'cause I figured I could find someone else to play it with. Beavis and Butt-head came up to me, which made me feel great because I was damn if I was going to crawl on my knees. Plus, we've done too much cool stuff together to let things get between us.

So then we played with Game Boy a minute and then Butt-head goes "this sucks", which I didn't agree with but which I sort of agreed with enough to go along with. So then we went over to the park and then Butt-head had the idea to trade it for 10 firecrackers.

I miss the Game Boy a little bit but it's cooler to hang out 'Cause I bet when I don't care about the Game Boy anymore I'll still be friends with Beavis and Butt-head.

Stewart

PLACE YOUR BETS

DAVID LEE ROTH **VS** VINCE NEIL

DAVID LEE ROTH SINGS LIKE A WUSS. HUH HUH,
BUT LIKE VINCE NEIL IS A WUSS.
YEAH, HEH HEH, DAVE KICKS VINCE'S ASS, AND
THEN METALLICA COMES AND LIGHTS HIM ON
FIRE DURING A CONCERT.
YEAH, HUH HUH, AND WE GET FREE TICKETS.
AND CHICKS, HUH HUH.

THIGH MASTER **VS** A LAWN MOWER

THIGH MASTER IS STRONG. IT'S GOT LIKE A
SPRING ON IT OR WHATEVER.
A LAWN MOWER COULD CUT IT UP REAL SMALL
AND SPRAY IT OUT.
YEAH.
THIGH MASTER IS A WUSS.

A SHARK **VS** A WHALE

A SHARK HAS TEETH.
YEAH, BUT A WHALE IS BIGGER THAN A SHARK.
UH, A SHARK IS SMARTER THAN A WHALE.
WHAT IF IT WAS A DOG? LIKE A DOG THAT
COULD SWIM VERSUS A WHALE.
IT WOULD KICK THE WHALE'S ASS.
WHAT IF IT WAS A SPERM WHALE?
HUH HUH HUH HUH HUH HUH HUH.
HEH HEH HEH HEH HEH M HEH HEH.

BLAZE FROM AMERICAN GLADIATOR **VS** DEATH TRUCK

DEATH TRUCK HAS LIKE A COMPUTER. THE
GOVERNMENT GAVE IT ARTIFICIAL
INTELEVISION.
YEAH. BUT BLAZE KICKS ASS.
YEAH, AND IF DEATH TRUCK IS SO SMART, I
WOULD TRY TO PICK UP BLAZE.
THEN SHE WOULD KICK ITS ASS AND DRIVE I
OVER HERE.
HUH HUH HUH. THAT WOULD BE COOL.

BUTT-HEAD **VS** A LION

THE LION IS SMARTER, HEH HEH.
SHUT UP, BEAVIS. I WOULD KICK HIS ASS AND
THEN TEAR HIS HEART OUT AND EAT IT.
LION HEART SUCKS. I'VE EATEN IT.
BEAVIS, YOU'RE FULL OF IT. IF THE LION
CLAWED ME, THOUGH, THAT WOULD BE COOL.
YEAH. SCARS ARE COOL.

BON JOVI **VS** A PIECE OF GRASS

BON JOVI WOULD SCREAM AT THE GRASS.
BUT THAT WOULD MAKE THE GRASS MAD.
YEAH, SO THEN IT WOULD LIKE HAVE TO
KICK HIS ASS. UH, BUT IF LIKE BON JOVI
AND RICHIE SAMBORA JUMPED THE GRASS
WHILE IT WAS SLEEPING, THEY MIGHT
HAVE A CHANCE.
THE GRASS WOULD STILL KICK THEIR ASSES.
YEAH.

VAN DRIESSEN **VS** ANDERSON

ANDERSON WAS LIKE IN WAR OF THE
WORLDS. PLUS, HE'S GOT LIKE A SAW.
NOT ANY MORE.
OH YEAH. HUH HUH.
PLUS VAN DRIESSEN WOULD SING A SONG.
ANDERSON WOULD DIE.
WHAT IF VAN DRIESSEN WAS A BEER?
THEN ANDERSON WOULD WIN.

VAN DAMME **VS** BEAVIS
WITH A SPEAR

THAT WOULD BE COOL.
YEAH, HEH HEH. A SPEAR WOULD KICK ASS.
NO IT WOULDN'T. VAN DAMME WOULD KICK
YOUR ASS.
NO HE WOULDN'T. I WOULD KICK HIS ASS.
HE'S GOT KARATE POWER. HE'D BREAK
YOUR SPEAR.
IF I HAD A LIGHTER, I WOULD KICK HIS ASS.
YEAH. YOU WOULD KICK HIS ASS THEN.

HOBBY CORNER

WOOD BURNING

FISHING

MODEL ROCKETRY

EMPTY LIGHTER COLLECTION

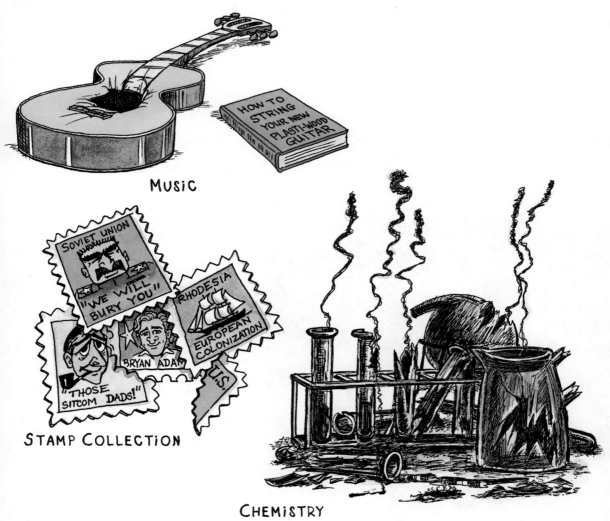

Music

Stamp Collection

Chemistry

Lepidoptery

DO'S AND DON'TS OF TEEN HYGIENE
BY BRADLEY BUZZCUT, U.S.M.C. (RET.)

If I had to boil my years of experience with teen young people into one lesson, it would be this: a life without hygiene is no life at all.

CORRECT

1. SELF-RESPECT The hygienic teen respects his self.

2. DISCIPLINE If self-respect is the soul of the hygienic teen, discipline is the skeleton. It holds the teen together like the bones of the body.

3. HAIR The first thing the hygienic teen asks his self each day is, "Is my hair an appropriate length for interaction with other members of my species?"

4. CLEANLINESS Teens are by their nature filthy of thought and body. But a clean body guards against a dirty mind— and cleanliness is next to second nature to the hygienic teen.

5. DRESS A neat presentation is the calling card of the hygienic teen. It is the look that says, "Hello, friend. I am a mature person who likes to help."

6. GAZE AND GRIP The hygienic teen offers the adults of his world a firm grip and good eye contact, for he is clean and has nothing to hide.

7. COMMUNICATION The hygienic teen presents his thoughts in crisp, clean sentences devoid of such verbal clutter as "uh" and "like."

An unhygienic attitude makes the body soft and vulnerable to moral unravelings. The two examples below offer you a simple choice: cleanliness or psychopath?

1. Without self-respect, the teen collapses into an animal-like state, slinking into shadow areas or parking lots, seeking the leadership of an Alpha-male who is most often a maggot, morals-wise.

2. The unhygienic teen has no discipline and therefore no bones and therefore allows his self to be shaped by the loud negative elements of his world: the rock singers, the hubcap stealers, and the grass puffers.

3. The unhygienic teen cares only for his self and gives not a hoot for the thoughts of others.

4. When the unhygienic teen allows the slime and offal of his world to accumulate under his nails, he also lets it gather deep inside his brain.

5. The clothes of the unhygienic teen say, "Stand back! I am a criminal and will harm you."

6. The unhygienic teen averts his gaze and does not proffer his hand in fellowship, for he is ashamed of his filth.

7. The unhygienic teen cannot organize his thoughts to make sense and freely peppers his conversations with relentless, maddening, nervous laughter.

BEAVIS: M HEH HEH. LET ME GET A TUBESTEAK AND A CHOCOLATE BUTT-SHAKE. HEH HEH.

BUTT-HEAD: HUH HUH HUH. IS THAT YOU, BEAVIS?

BEAVIS: HEY, BUTT-HEAD. DO YOU THINK YOU'LL EVER, LIKE, GET MARRIED?

BUTT-HEAD: UH, ARE YOU PROPOSING, DUDE?

BEAVIS: NO, THIS IS SOMEBODY ELSE, ASSWIPE. HEH HEH.	BUTT-HEAD: THEN PULL UP TO THE WINDOW, SIR. YOUR ORDER WILL BE READY IN A MINUTE.

BEAVIS: NO.	BUTT-HEAD: THAT'S OK, I'D ONLY MARRY SOMEBODY DUMB ANYWAY. HUH HUH.

How to Make a Million $

Sell your blood

Invent something

Make somebody pay you not to blow up something

Discover oil like Jed Clampett

Wear like a tie

Sell T-shirts at concerts

Make up one of those incommercials

Look for change with a metal detector

Kick the asses of the guys who are beating up a rich dude. Then the dude leaves you money when he croaks. Cool.

Sell your sperm

Write a book.

How to Spend It

A truckload of M-100's and some jugs of subscription cold medicine

A satellite dish

Pay-per-view

Buy like Metallica to come play for you at your house

A big home-video control room

Have like a water tower full of nacho sauce

Hire a guy to change the remote for you

Take a limo to school. Then trash it.

Buy a lot of cool videos

Get some of those Air Jordan sneakers that massage your feet. Only they're made of gold.

A couch that has like automatic beverages

HEY, BEAVIS. 'MEMBER WHEN WE WERE LIKE YOUNG AND, UH, FAMOUS OR WHATEVER? AND WE WERE ON TEE-SHIRTS AND HATS AND LIKE ON TV AND IN BOOKS AND CRAP?

HEH HEH. YEAH.

THAT WAS COOL.

WHAT'S THAT?

THAT WAS COOL.

SCHOOL?

THAT WAS COOL, ASS WIPE.

HEH HEH. NO IT WASN'T. SCHOOL SUCKED.

Uh-knowledge Mints

Uh, like writing a book sucks.
Yeah. Heh heh. It's like worse than reading one.
We couldn't of done it alone.
Yeah. We needed a lot of help screwing it up. Heh heh.
Uh, this is the part where like we knowledge who helped us.
Yeah. These are the knowledge mints, heh heh.
It's Uh-Knowledge Mints, dumb ass.
Oh yeah.
I.M. Horny. Huh huh. And Anita Hanchob.
Heh heh. Yeah. Hugh G. Rection and Dick Hertz. Heh heh m heh heh.
Phil McCreviss. Huh huh.
Heh heh. Jack Mehoff.
Harry Johnson and uh, S. Munch. Huh huh.
I.M. Horny. Heh heh.
You already said that, Beavis.
Oh yeah. Um, Pepe Roni. Heh heh. Yeah. Pepe Roni.
Lotte Nockers. Huh huh. And Dick Weed. And uh, Ima Hogg.
Um, I.M. Horny. No, wait, another one. Um, Frank Furter. Heh heh,
yeah, Frank Furter.
That's stupid.
You're stupid.
No. You are.
Heh heh m heh heh.
Huh huh huh huh huh.
This is cool.
Yeah. This is cool.